名流詩叢 8

愛之頌 Song of Love

Cânt de iubir

〔羅馬尼亞〕Elena Liliana Popescu◎著

李魁賢◎中譯　〔美〕Adrian George Sahlean◎英譯

當前往
寂靜的國度
詩人為我們留下
一首愛之頌

作者簡介

　　波佩斯古1948年生，羅馬尼亞詩人，數學博士，執教於母校布加勒斯特大學。1994年以詩集《給你》（Tie）登上詩壇。接著出版《思想間的版圖》（Târâmul dintre Gânduri, 1997），《愛之頌》（Cânt de Iubire，1999）、《歌頌存在》（Imu Existentei, 2000）和《朝聖》（Pelerin, 2003）。《如果》（Dacâ, 2007）一書只有一首詩，卻收二十六種語言譯本，其中漢語是李魁賢所譯。她本身也是翻譯家，把李魁賢的《溫柔的美感》詩集譯成羅馬尼亞文出版。

譯　序

　　2006年春節遠道前往拉丁美洲的尼加拉瓜，參加第二屆格瑞納達國際詩歌節。格瑞納達古城樸素的氣氛，令人充分放鬆心情，享受浮生偷閒的樂趣。拉丁美洲諸多國家通用西班牙語，國際聚會幾乎不需透過翻譯，便可彼此瞭解，真是便利極了，可是對不諳西班牙語的人，就有無異被擱在圈外的感覺。於是，少數來自非西班牙語系國家的詩人，彼此自然而然便有較多接觸機會。

　　波佩斯古（Elena Liliana Popescu）似乎因此和我比較多交談，她來自羅馬尼亞，正好我在2002年去旅行過，無形中又增加話題。波佩斯古是一位數學教授，屬於木訥型的學者，所以談話間令人感到態度誠懇。經互贈詩集後，因詩歌節期間比較清閒，又無

旁騖，正好可以好整以暇地閱讀，見面時又可互道感想，故頗為相得。

回國後不久，接到她寄來把我的幾首詩譯成羅馬尼亞文，我當即以漢語譯她的四首詩回報，並發表在台灣日報副刊。過不久，她把拙著《溫柔的美感》全部五十首詩譯完，也找到Pelerin出版社出書，算是行動派的人物，甚至還熱心向古巴政府主辦的國際詩歌節推薦邀我參加。

在國際詩交流上，有輸出也要有輸入，才能產生真正互通的成果，於是我也把她的詩集《愛之頌》（Cânt de Iubire）根據Adrian George Sahlean的英譯本（Song of Love）全譯成漢語，打成私印本寄給她，但遷延三年，迄今才得以正式出版，了卻一份詩交流平衡的願望。

波佩斯古的詩簡短精要，或許因數學純理性的訓練，這些短詩也有理性勝於感性的傾向。就個別言，可藉此看出數理邏輯人才寫詩風格之一斑，就全體言，何嘗不可在此管中窺豹，體會在台灣不為人知的

羅馬尼亞詩人作品的一鱗半爪，由此心靈之窗，透視遙遠的陌生國度的不同文學表現，正可開拓我們無限的詩領域。

2009.09.29

目次

目次

愛之頌

如果你只知道

如果祢只知道

我多麼懷念祢

雖然祢常在我心裡

我多麼傷心

只能在我夢中

看到祢

我多麼想祢

雖然祢始終與我同在……

痛苦有多深

只能在我思念裡

聽見祢

多麼難受啊

當我環顧搜尋祢

只能在祢想要現身時

才能找到祢

If you only knew

If You only knew,

how much I yearn for You,

though You're in my heart!

How great the sadness

to see You

only in my dream.

I miss You so,

though You're with me always...

How deep the pain

to hear You

only in my thoughts.

How hard it is

when I seek You

and find You only

when You want to be found.

你已漂流

你已漂流在雜念間

離開你的初衷

直到你再回頭

卻不能決定去留……

You've drifted

You've drifted among other thoughts

Far from the first one,

And till you return,

You can neither leave nor stay...

我不曉得有多正直

我不曉得自己有多正直

能夠以瞭解變成誤解

所扭曲的心情來批判

你完美創造的世界？

How right am I, I wonder?

How right am I, I wonder?

to judge with mind distorted

by faulty understanding

in a World created perfect?

不明白

多少折衝妥協

才能使熱心的人

為輕微的快樂動搖——

他不明白在經過時

丟在腦後

斷橋的深淵

總有一天需要跨越

Without knowing

How many compromises

A man makes eagerly

for the smallest pleasure ——

unaware it passes

leaving behind

a bridgeless abyss

he must cross some day.

猶豫的時刻

你仍然在遠方……

路途遙遠

漫步在

選擇的流刑地

於猶豫的時刻

在生死之間

永恆

In a suspended moment

You're still afar...

Long is the path

traveled

in this exile

chosen, in a suspended moment

between death and life

Eternal.

我寫給你

我寫給你一封信

放在我心裡

時時刻刻

你會收到

每次

都回信

——難道我會

弄錯——

今天

明天

或許永不……

I write You

I write You a letter

in my mind,

now and again.

You receive it

and answer

every time—

or, am I wrong

perhaps—

Today,

tomorrow,

may be never...

無人回答

偶爾

你自問

生命是什麼

並不真正

急於

找到

答案……

所以你永遠找不到!

但無人

回答

因為

無人會有

答案……

Nobody answered

At times,

You asked yourself

' What's life? '

not really

eager

for

an answer...

And so you never found it!

No one

answered

because

no one

could have...

或者也許

會是因為自私

逼迫你

攀登狹路

拱你高高

在上？

或者也許　你心裡

說　杯已滿

而你的愛

滿溢

是你所提供？

Can it be, perhaps

Can it be, perhaps, selfishness

compelling you

to the narrow paths

that take you

ever higher?

Or, can it be, perhaps, your heart

saying: the cup was full,

and your love

overflowed

when you offered it?

所以我們會出生

在我們一生中死過

幾次

我們都不知道

所以我們會重新出生

生命是由無數瞬間組成

然則有多少才能測量死亡？……

So we'll be born

How many times in our life

we die

and we don't even know,

so we'll be born anew

Life's made of countless instants,

how many, though, will measure death?...

告訴我

　　如果火焰迷途

　　一剎那間

　　燒掉受苦蒼蠅

　　脆弱的翅翼

　　受了傷　　明知

　　在光的庇護下

　　痛苦會持續

　　告訴我　　要怪誰？

Tell me

And if a flame errs from its way

an instant,

and burns the fragile wing

of a pained fly

And suffers, for it knows

that wrapping it in light,

the pain will grow,

Tell me, who is to blame?

夢想家

如果我周圍所見

不是生活

那麼何處是真正

生活所在？

怯怯詢問

冰柱

在衰敗的世界裡

做夢……

Dreamer

If what I see around me

isn't life

Then where is life

for real?

Asked, timidly,

an icicle,

dreaming,

in a perishing world...

我要遠行

我要遠行

到另一國土

但

一回首

我不願

留下

純真的生命

那

只能因我的愛

獲得安慰

I would go far away

I would go far away

into another Realm,

but,

looking back,

I would not like

to leave behind

innocent beings

who

could be consoled

by my love alone.

我怎麼啦？

你第一次離開我

沒有回首

你怎麼啦

如今　我提醒你

你早已遺忘

我怎麼啦？

What's with me?

You leave me for the first time

without looking back.

What's with you?

And now, I am reminding you

you've forgotten.

What's with me?

你自問

來自天堂的天使

有兇惡的臉孔

露出笑容說

愛！

來自地獄的惡魔

有天使的臉孔

叫出你的格調

愛！

在你內心裡

那些聲音糾葛

迴響著
愛！

從朦朧昨日
幽幽深處
於今陽光普照
聽到聲音
愛！

對　你也可以聽到
你自問
愛嗎？

You ask yourself

An angel from Heaven

with a demon face

shows up and says:

Love!

A demon from Hell

with an angel face,

calls out your way:

Love!

Inside you,

their voice entwined,

resound:

Love!

And from the depth

of that dim yesterday,

now lit up by the sun,

a voice is heard:

Love!

Yes, you can hear it too,

And now you ask yourself:

Am I in love?

我　願

我願

凝望祢

山巒矗立面前

視若砂粒

單藉祢的光

就能引導我上路

走向光明……

然則

上帝啊

我能克服

漸消的苦痛

我的淚眼

盈眶

凝視我自己

再度發現

永遠　純粹

I wish

I wish,

looking at You,

that the mountains rising before me

were grains of sand

and Your light alone

would guide me on the path

towards Light...

Then,

oh God,

I could vanquish

my consuming pain,

and my eyes,

tearful now,

would look at myself,

found again,

forever, pure.

生命在夢中

融化的蠟燭

仍然燃燒

瞬間

沒有火焰……

終於

知道

時間如何

測量生命

在夢中

Life in the dream

A melting candle

still burns

an instant

without a flame...

knowing

at last

how Time

measures lives

in the Dream.

連　續

銀色小蝴蝶啊

多麼晶瑩的歌聲

隨著妳飛翔！

泡沫透明的白蝴蝶啊

在水晶花朵之間

忙碌……

妳的遊戲多麼短暫！

渴極的陽光

把妳飲盡……

妳的死亡會賦予新生命

使遊戲繼續……

一齣火焰

在灰燼花朵之間

飛翔……

Continuity

Little butterflies of silver,

How crystalline the song

Along your flight!

White butterflies of foam translucent,

running from flower to

crystal flower...

How short's your play!

A thirsty ray of sun

will drink you up...

Your death will give new life

So that the play go on...

A play of flames

flying from flower to flower

of embers...

只有你的容貌

我在心中聚集如許多的美
從未來的世紀　從古老的世紀
從你無法分辨的成千容貌
只有你的容貌我已在模中成型

你的笑臉真實　但純粹到
神永遠無法照亮或存在
遠遠看著你　在藍天下
我的心默默私語你就是祂

Your face alone

I've gathered so much beauty in my heart

From centuries to come, from centuries of old,

And out of thousand faces you can't tell apart

Your face alone I've shaped into a mold.

Your smiling face was real, but so pure

As gods could never shine or be,

And, seeing you an instant, under the sky azure,

My heart in silence whispered you were He.

夢中意象

妳的眼中

露出翡翠

純粹水晶淚

像妳的笑容！

妳的淡黃秀髮

披在肩上

框著一張臉

有天使的眼睛！

啊　妳是如此之美

從我的想像誕生

要妳來對我相望

告訴我　妳傳達

什麼訊息？

Image in dream

Your eyes seep

emeralds,

pure tears of crystal.

As you smile!

Your flaxen tresses

overflow the shoulders,

framing a Face of

eyes angelic !

Oh, you're so beautiful,

born out of my thoughts,

Have you come to look at me.

Tell me, what

you're heralding?

疑　惑

如果不怕

別人會做得更好

好得多

我們要說歎為觀止

我們自己做主

一切生計

為我們而起

讚美令人滿意的幸福

可是我們怕

甚至怕對抗恐懼……

Mistrust

Were it not for fear

that someone else would do it better,

much better,

we'd say wonderful things,

and we'd be masters of ourselves,

and all Living

would raise for us

Hymns to a happiness fulfilled.

But we are fearful,

Even to fight our fear...

負　義

一片雪花

在陽光下融化

轉化成

千朵火焰

以嚇人的

寒冷

飲盡對它

仰慕的海……

Ingratitude

A snow flake

melted in the sun

and turned into

a thousand flames

And then, with terrifying

coldness,

Drank up the sea

that longed for it...

轉　型

步伐跟隨著步伐

時間衝出時間！

混沌迷失於混沌……

遺忘

重現於知識內

於知悉之前

光明佔領黑暗！

黑暗打破光明……

宇宙傾向無涯

無涯

變成有限

沉默領先於喧嘩……

曲線交叉直線

直線交叉曲線

圓　圓　圓

線折斷　線拉直

線彎曲　筆直

點　點　點

Transformation

Steps follow steps,

Time rushes out time!

Chaos is lost in chaos...

Oblivion

is found again within the knowledge

Before knowing.

Light fills the darkness!

Darkness breaks the light...

The universe tends to the infinite,

The infinite

becomes finite.

Silence precedes the noise...

Curves intersect the lines,

Lines intersect the curves,

And circles, circles, circles.

Lines broken and lines straight,

Curved lines, and lines,

Point. Dot. Period.

我要試試

我要試試醒來

如今

當夢正在消失……

I'll try

I'll try to wake up,

now

when dreams are vanishing...

然後呢？

我但願能從幸運花

收集眾多花瓣

可是那永恆的夢想

仍然保留完整……

然則我但願能

啜其露水

可是整個太陽

耽留在內

加以吸飲

我會被熱火耗竭

And then?

I wish I could gather petals

From the flower of happiness.

But its eternal dream

Is to remain whole...

I wish then I could sip

its dew.

But the entire sun

dwells within,

and drinking it

I'd be consumed by flames.

向　妳

小星星

在遠方照耀

使人們可以

看到妳的亮麗

妳召喚我

閃閃不停

妳想念我

啊　但願我有能力前來

看我正長出翅膀

我沖天

飛向妳

無所畏懼！

Toward you

Little star,

Who shine afar

So people

Can see your brightness.

You beckon to me to join you.

Blinking so often.

Do you miss me?

Oh, were it in my power to come!

But look, wings are growing on me.

And I can soar

and fly toward you,

And I fear no one!

聖殤石雕

眼睛正看透純大理石

歌唱無可比擬的愛

承受永恆的絕念

滿懷痛苦為世界搖籃

空間縮小而後時間消失

大理石獨自默默流淚⋯⋯

自然靜寂　絕望揮之不去

生死何時該要求獻祭

人類整體如今已告迷失

透過此無限且徹底譴責

連聖母馬利亞都單獨

祈求我們的寬容

上天慈悲而後恩寵隨到

只有大理石栩栩如生

聖像永恆　為祢所雕刻

祢的憐憫使者神聖自在

Pietà

The eyes are piercing the pure marble

That sings the love beyond compare

It bears in its eternal resignation

The full pain cradling the World.

Space shrinks and then, Time disappears

Alone the marble weeps in silence...

And Nature's quiet, for despair lingers

When death from life her tribute has to ask.

Mankind entire is now lost

Through this immense

and overwhelming blame

Even the Virgin solely prays

For our Forgiveness.

Heaven relents and then Grace comes,

Only the marble is alive.

Icon eternal, sculpted by You,

Herald of Your Pity divine.

門開著

自由是通道

自由的是知識

通到偉大

王國的門

那裡有多樣思想

匯集

等候了

無數年代

要走進

門……

Open is the gate

Free is the passage

and free the Knowledge

toward the Gate

of the great kingdom

where multitudes of thoughts

gather

after they've waited

through ages

to walk in

the Gate...

找到你時

海洋的自由受到海岸約制

最漆黑的幽暗仍含有光

靜寂的陸地怕洶湧的浪濤

退潮時只留下未來的世界

在你不朽之後一切似乎空無

在此無聲的絕望中世界寂然

不幸本身擁有著幸福

在你謙卑　要離開世間之時

被壓抑的妄想隱藏真理

在你離去時才會澄清

而今天不過是鏡花水月

在找到你時卻變成永恆……

When you are found

The ocean's freedom's reined in by the shore,

The fullest darkness still contains the light

The land of stillness fears the moving wave

That leaves behind it, when it's gone,

    only the world to come

And all seems nothing when immortality

    you're after

And in this mute despair the word is silent

Unhappiness itself holds happiness within

When, humbled, you will leave this world.

Subdued illusion hides the truth

Only to make it clear when you depart

That which today is transitory

And turns eternal when you're found.

原諒我

原諒我

空白頁

打破你的寧靜

以低聲細語

佈置

一行又

一行

追探我的思想

運作

尋思

且搜查

不知

其存在

不知

其隱藏

我的寧靜

和你的

Forgive me

Forgive me

blank page

for breaking your tranquility

with whispers

laid out

line after

line,

tracing thoughts of mine,

that run

seeking

and searching

without knowing

they exist,

without knowing

they conceal

my Tranquility

and yours.

我看不出

我一向的理由

錯了

我竟然看不出

多簡單

可以超越

I couldn't see

I have used reason:

A mistake,

And I couldn't see

How simple it can be,

Beyond it.

我獨自

我坐著看海

一望無際

我全然獨自

海鷗

（我喚醒的思想）

棲息在岸上

遠遠　一點

（未道的思想）

等候

海浪來了又去

或大或小　或喜或悲

歌聲　輕聲細語

帶我到

迷人的世界

片刻

靜極了

聽到神祕的交響樂

發自內心

即使海在面前

一望無際

海浪

靜默的歌聲

完美無缺……

By myself

I sit and watch the sea

and it looks boundless.

All by myself.

Seagulls

-thoughts awaken by me-

rest on the shore.

Far off, a dot

-a thought as yet unspoken-

awaits.

Waves come and go,

Big and small, happy and sad.

Their song, a whisper hushed,

carries me

to their enchanted world.

For a while.

So much silence!

The mysterious symphony is heard

From within.

Even the Sea is there.

Boundless.

With waves

whose silent song

is perfect...

你沒告訴過我

你告訴過我

詩

像是

前所未見……

奇蹟

發現在

靜默的時刻

隱藏在

通常的

事實裡

你告訴過我

詩

奇妙無比

內部保持

絕望

無法洞悉

神秘

但你沒告訴過我

詩

呼喚你

何處

可找到

問題和答案

You never told me

You told me

Poetry

is like

nothing ever before...

A miracle

found

in the silent moment

that lies hidden

in the common

fact.

You told me

Poetry

is Wonderment

that holds within

despair

for not knowing

the Mystery.

But you never told me

Poetry

calls you

Where

you can find

The Question-Answer

我們會討論沉默

我知道

沒有比沉默

更好

敘說

何謂死

何謂生……

只要你停留！

我們會談論

沉默

且更加

明白

內心的

沉默

我知道

沒有比沉默

更好

充實

時刻

苦惱

言語……

We would have talked silences

I know of

nothing better

than Silence

to say

what's death,

what's life...

If you'd have only stayed!...

We would've talked

silences

and known

better

that Silence

within ourselves.

I know of

nothing better

than Silence

to fill up

the moment,

the suffering,

the word...

省視你內心

我在何處　這個人在問

全部世界上的科學

無法給我答案？

省視你內心！

你就在那裡　今天的你

等候你的本身自我

明天的你　昨天的你……

Look into your heart

Where am I, the one who's asking,

While all the world's science

Cannot answer me?

Look into your heart!

You are there, the one of today,

Waiting for your own self,

the one of tomorrow, of yesterday...

你不會孤單

時間近了

在你內心的堡壘

你是真正

自由

你不難從鏡子

凝視你雜亂的

影像

被時空

扭曲

你會知道

你非其中一員

你與自己同在

而你不再

孤單

You will not be alone

The time is near when,

within the fortress of your heart,

you're truly

free.

You'll look untroubled

at your sundry images

from mirrors,

distorted

by time and space,

And you'll know

you're not any of them.

Then you'll be with Yourself

and you'll no longer be

alone.

給　你

迄今我不敢說

會真正

自由

因為我不知道

我的自由

有何作為

如今我知道

我必須把它貢獻

給祢

以絕對的服從

To you

Until today, I have not dared

to be truly

free

because I didn't know

what to do

with my freedom.

I know now

I must offer it

to You,

in absolute submission.

愛之頌

坐在沉默桌前

於未知的國度

詩人為我們

撕開新鮮麵包

灑著

天堂露……

據說死者跟死者

生者跟生者！

可是我們真正知道

誰是死者

誰是生者？

多一位詩人

在外⋯⋯

少一位詩人

在此

當前往

寂靜的國度

詩人為我們留下

一首愛之頌

無人知⋯⋯

Song of Love

Seated at the table of Silence,

in unknown kingdom,

Poets break for us

fresh bread,

that's sprinkled

with the Dew of Heaven...

They say the dead go with the dead,

the living with the living!

But do we really know

who are the dead,

and who the living?

A Poet more,

beyond...

A poet less,

in here.

When parting

for the silent kingdom,

the Poet leaves with us

a song of Love

unknown...

時間　何往呢？

我錯了

沒讓愛情

像河流……

時間　何往呢？

回來讓我

完成我的語句！

Time, where have you gone?

I have been wrong

not to let love

flow like a river...

Time, where have you gone?

Come back and let me

carry my sentence out!

那　裡

我們每人能過的
生活是多麼美麗啊
看似遙遠
卻還是那麼近……

我們每人遭遇的
痛苦是多麼深
熱烈又純淨
我們真的會……

我們每人能走的
路途是多麼短
始終帶領每人
到達其本真之處

There

How beautiful that life

We each could live,

So far

And yet so near...

How deep the pain

We each could suffer,

Burning and purifying,

So we can truly be...

How short the path

We each could walk

That always brings each one

To where one really is.

我看見她

我看見她到來

無論是否預料中

無論是緩緩或突然

她得意洋洋離去

或自以為得意

因為她能取的

只是她所能帶的

只是她會失落的

每次她注意到

有別人先在

而且一如此刻知道

她賦有權力

只有如此她才能順從

悄悄帶著

此項知識的負擔

在生命永恆之際

I saw her

I saw her arrive,

Expected or not,

Slow or suddenly.

And she leaves victoriously,

Or so she thinks,

For she can take

Only what she can carry,

Only what can be lost.

Each time she notices

Someone Else was there first

And understands, as now,

She was given power

Only so she can obey,

And carry quietly

The burden of this knowledge

During Life eternal.

確　實

在死亡之上

愛把存在

弄成非存在

就在通過遺忘時！

而超越了生命

已知和未知

以永恆的公平

奔馳越過心靈

生命本身歇憩

已悟和未悟

他是永遠

在追尋的那人

Certainty

It is above death

Love that takes

Being into non-being

When it passes into oblivion!

And beyond that life

Known and unknown

That runs across the soul

With eternal candor,

Lies Life itself,

Fathomed and unfathomed

By he who's on

Eternal quest.

自　從

自從那情況

放空一切不是祢

自從祢讓我

凝望超越我自己

而且看到祢

要讓我看到的事

自從我　永遠的旅人

謙卑於探尋往年

並且倦於

自以為我所負的重擔

我已坐在妄想的

十字路口

等待祢的恩寵

Ever since

Ever since that instance

Emptied of everything that is not You,

Ever since You let me

Look beyond myself

And see what You

Would let me see,

Ever since, I, eternal passenger,

Humbled in my quest of yesteryear

And tired

of the burden I thought I carried,

I've sat at the crossroads

Of illusions

Awaiting Your grace.

超 越

超越
變與不變
動與靜

超越
多樣和獨一
言語和沉默

超越
愚與智
不在與存在

只剩下你

Beyond

Beyond

change and permanence,

movement and stillness,

Beyond

diversity and uniqueness,

word and silence,

Beyond

ignorance and knowledge,

non-being and existence,

It's only you.

只有透過實存

我知道　只有透過沉默

你可以說出真理

也知道　只有透過死亡

你可以真正活著

我知道　只有透過痛苦

你可以克服苦難

也知道　只有透過損失

你可以維持勝利

我知道　只有透過愛

你測試存在

也知道　只有透過實存

你可以變成自由

Through being only

I know, only through silence

you can say the truth.

And also know, through dying only

You can truly live.

I know, only through pain

you conquer suffering.

And also know, through losing only

you can stay a winner.

I know, only through love

you test existence.

And also know, through being only

you can become free.

不可能

我並不隨時有靈感

去描述祢的偉大

可是當我有了靈感

我知道那是無法描述的……

我並不隨時有靈感

去塗繪祢的影像

可是當我有了靈感

我知道那是無法塗繪的……

我並不隨時有靈感

去歌詠祢的榮光

可是當我有了靈感

我知道那是無法歌詠的……

The impossible

I'm not inspired at all times

to describe Your greatness

But when I am,

I know it cannot be described...

I'm not inspired at all times

to portray Your image

But when I am,

I know it cannot be portrayed...

I'm not inspired at all times

to sing Your glory

But when I am,

I know it cannot be sung...

一刻也不

太陽啊　你在何處

要是不在我心中

你由此出發

或升

或沉

一刻也不

缺席？

世界啊　你在何處

要是不在我心中

你由此出發

或成

或敗

一刻也不
缺席？

心啊　你在何處
要是不在我心中
你由此出發
或生
或死
一刻也不
缺席？

存在啊　你是誰
要是不在我心中

一切由此出發

或現

或逝

一刻也不

消失？

Not even an instant

Where are you, oh, sun

If not within my Heart,

From where you take leave

To rise

And set,

Yet never absent

Even an instant?

Where are you, oh, world

If not within my Heart,

From where you take leave

To create

And destroy yourself,

Yet never absent

Even an instant?

Where are you, oh, heart

If not within my Heart,

From where you take leave

To be born

And die,

Yet never absent

Even an instant?

Who are you, oh, existence

If not my Heart,

From where everything leaves

To appear

And disappear,

Yet never ceasing to be

Even an instant?

不知不覺

我迄今

了無遺憾

已歷數世紀

當你讓我相信

我夠格擁有

一切世界的喜樂

不知不覺

我真的領受了

身為祢的子女

Unware

How ungrateful

I have been

for many centuries,

when you let me believe

I'm entitled

to all the world's joys,

unaware

I truly deserve them

as Your son.

我凝視自己

我凝視自己在

永恆國度的鏡中

但我只看到

祢的臉

對我顯現

所以我認識祢

當我發覺

我是祢的影像

I looked at myself

I looked at myself in the mirror

of the timeless realm

but I only saw

Your face,

which You gave to me

so I can recognize You

when I become aware

that I am in Your image.

我承認祢

我承認祢

以祢母親的影像

她把血液給我

使我能夠出生

給我搖籃歌

使我能夠成長

還有她的生命

使我能夠理解

我承認祢

以我兒子的影像

他把坦率給我

使我可以再生

給我夢想

使我重新找到自己

還有他的叛逆

使我能夠理解

我承認祢

以我朋友的影像

他把力量給我

使我能夠堅持

給我希望

使我能夠一起完成

還有他的冷靜

使我能夠理解

只有當

我承認祢

以我老師的影像

他把祢的達理給我

使我能夠知己

還有祢的愛

使我能夠理解

以及祢的沉默

所以我「在」……

I recognized you

I recognized You

in the image of my mother,

who gave me her blood

so I can be born,

her cradle song

so I can grow.

and her life

so I can understand,

I recognized You

in the image of my son,

who gave me his candor

so I can be born anew,

his dreams

so I can find myself again,

and his rebelliousness,

so I can understand,

I recognized You

in the image of my friend,

who gave me his strength

so I can go on,

his hopes

so we can fulfill them together,

and his indifference,

so I can understand,

Only when

I recognized You

in the image of my Teacher,

who gave me Your understanding

so I can know myself,

Your love

so I can understand,

and Your silence,

so I can Be...

當

坦率不會老

當自由

隱藏服從

使沉默退位

當虛榮

不能入侵

祕密的神廟

When

Candor is ageless

When freedom

Hides obedience

That silent resignation,

When vanity

Can not invade

The secret shrines.

朝向自己

我漫步走過夢世界

單獨　朝向我自己

守在一旁再三思量

超出無數思量的海域

清澈　在表現的無量中

我到達自己的陽光海岸

在此我始終是

永恆　幸福　不動搖……

Toward myself

I wander though the world of dreams

Alone, towards my own self,

Setting aside thought after thought

Out of the sea of thoughts untold.

Lucid, in the apparent immensity,

I reach the sunlit shore of myself,

Where I have always been

Eternal, happy, immovable...

我相信

我相信

什麼原因變化

正如我相信什麼保持其

連續

我相信

什麼誕生繁榮

正如我相信其中必有的

智慧

我相信

什麼創造多元

正如我相信單獨存在的

獨特

我相信

什麼生成話語

正如我相信擁抱一切的

　　　　沉默

我相信

什麼超越善惡

正如我相信大愛超越了

　　　　愛情

我相信

什麼存乎一心

正如我相信「存在」超越了

　　　　存在

愛之頌　　155

I believe

I believe

in what causes change,

As I believe in what keeps its

                    continuity;

I believe

in what gives birth to exuberance,

As I believe in the wisdom

                    within it;

I believe

in what creates diversity,

As I believe in the unique that exists

                    alone;

I believe

in what fathers the word,

As I believe in the silence that

> *embraces everything;*

I believe

in what's beyond evil and good,

As I believe in Love

> *beyond love;*

I believe

in what exists in each and every being,

As I believe in Existence beyond

> *existence.*

如 果

如果你能

測所未測

介入無涯

走過空無

非此即彼

如果你能

無愛之愛

無望之望

無言之言

無思之思

如果你能

聞所未聞

見所未見

知所未知

何來新肇

If

If you could ever

Measure the immeasurable,

Take in the boundlessness

And, walking across nothingness,

Be neither one or the other;

If you could ever

Be love without loving ,

Be hope without hoping ,

Be speech without speaking,

Be thinking without thinking;

If you could ever

Hear the unheard,

Look into the unseen

And learn the unknown,

Would there be a new beginning?

為何？

為何那麼多言語

在尋找

什麼是背後的意義？

為何那麼多前言

去學習

什麼是必要的？

為何那麼多超載

去發現

什麼是載量不足？

為何需要知道

什麼只靠遺忘

就有助於你的知識？

為何希望

你能夠得到

不缺的東西？

為何這是革命？

或許只是想自己

找到和平……

Why?

Why so many words

to seek

what's behind them?

Why so much foreword

to learn

what's necessary?

Why so much overload

to discover

what's under?

Why the need to know

what only by forgetting

would help your knowledge?

Why hope

for what only not wanting

you could get?

Why this revolt?

Perhaps only to find peace

With myself...

我發現自己

我時時刻刻害怕空虛

以及仍然受苦的那些人

周圍深深的悲傷

還有我　當我忘了我是誰

我時時刻刻害怕自己

因為自己的愚昧

相信我能夠改變

世界如夢似幻的浩瀚

我時時刻刻害怕時間

以及空間的衝擊

但我發現自己煥然一新

在自我寧靜的時刻

I find myself again

I'm scared at times by the void

And the deep sadness

Of those around who still suffer,

And mine, when I forget who I am.

I'm scared at times by myself

When, in my ignorance,

I believe I can change

The world's illusory immensity.

I'm scared at times be Time,

And the clash with Space

But I find myself anew

In the moment of peace with myself.

有一天

有一天　鳥飛入

我的心中……

從此　我長出翅膀

學會唱歌

開始飛翔……

衝向天空多美妙

呼吸芬芳空氣

在陽光下翱翔

多麼美哉……

One day

One day, a bird entered

my heart...

Since then, I've grown wings,

Learned to sing,

Started to fly...

How beautiful to soar to the sky

How good to breathe

the scented air,

And fly beneath the sun rays...

教 我

教我如何能夠

在人生道上

不需任何事物

以免造成負擔

教我如何行走

在苦難當中

於快樂時候

洋洋自得

在自我的路途上

教我　因此

能夠寬恕

像祢

Teach me

Teach me to be able

not to desire anything

of what can be a burden

on my way to the Path.

Teach me to walk on,

among the suffering

and happy times,

triumphant,

on the road to myself.

Teach me, therefore,

to be able to forgive,

like You.

找到祢

我開始走上

未走過的路途

攀登朝向我自己

下坡的階梯

我跑離躺在我

外面的無常

所以我可以找到祢

祢始終就是我

To find you

I started on the path

I'd never taken,

to climb stairs coming down

towards myself.

I ran away from the ephemeral

lying outside Me,

so I can find You

Who has always been Me.

答 案

存在或不存在？

那是問題

即世界已嘗試回答

透過所遴選者

雖然據說每人

會被遴選一次

存在或不存在

這是答案

即世界依然等待

透過獲遴選者

在自己內心

自問

Answer

To be or not to be?

That is the question

That the world has tried to answer

Through the chosen one,

Though, it is said, each one

Will be chosen once.

To Be and not to be.

This is the answer

That the world still awaits

Through the Chosen one,

When it quests

within itself.

轉變成愛

詩人多麼年輕啊

他誤解愛的欲望

隱士多麼聰明啊

他嘗試藉愛苦修

愛只不過是

對美的夢想

剩留下來的

只是傷心的巨浪……

苦修雕琢的真珠

在飄泊的心靈中

你會攜帶進入

祕密的境界

浪已退潮

在無動於中的春天

妳剩留下來

轉變成愛……

Turned into love

How young can be the poet

Who mistakes lust for love

How wise the hermit

Who tries on suffering through love.

Love is nothing

But a dream about beauty

That leaves behind

Mere heavy waves of sadness...

Suffering carves pearls

In your wandering soul

That you'll carry over

The secret boundary.

The waves have receded

In the spring still untouched

And you are left behind

Turned into love...

我懇求你

我懇求你

治癒我的愚昧

那妨礙我學習

我所知

我懇求你

治癒我的虛弱

那妨礙我學習

我所能

我懇求你

治癒我的自私

那妨礙我學習
我自謙

我懇求你
治癒我的盲目
那妨礙我學習
我所見

我懇求你
隱藏我的外貌
那妨礙我學習
我所是

I beg you

I beg of you,

to heal my ignorance

which prevents me from learning

that I know.

I beg of you,

to heal my powerlessness

which prevents me from learning

that I can.

I beg of you,

to heal my selfishness

which prevents me from learning

that I am humble.

I beg of you,

to heal my blindness

which prevents me from learning

that I see.

I beg of you,

to hide the appearance

which prevents me from learning

that I Am.

跟我來！

你何不遠走高飛

且霎時遺忘

你是如何無辜和傷心？

你何不展望

超越自己

且真心與我相見？

丟棄你破爛的衣服

跟我來

單獨籠罩在光明中！

你曾想家

但你一直讓人盼望

你不知道嗎？

Come with me!

Why won't you soar

and forget for an instant

how ignorant and sad you are?

Why won't you look

beyond yourself

and meet me, in truth?

Leave your worn out clothes behind

and come with me,

wrapped in Light alone!

You're ever homesick,

but you have been awaited,

did you not know!

我是心肝

我來到你心中

我長久在你心中

我從未離開到別處

只留在你心中

你來到我心中

你長久在我心中

你從未離開到別處

只留在我心中

我是我的心肝

我是

I am my heart

I came into your heart.

I've been a long time in your heart.

I've never been elsewhere

But in your heart.

You came into my heart.

You've been a long time in my heart.

You've never been elsewhere

But in my heart.

I am my Heart.

I am.

國家圖書館出版品預行編目

愛之頌 / 波佩斯古（Elena Liliana Popescu）著；
　李魁賢中譯；Adrian George Sahlean英譯. -- 一
版. -- 臺北市：秀威資訊科技, 2010. 01
　　面；　公分. --（語言文學類；PG0306）
BOD版
中英對照
譯自：Song of love
ISBN 978-986-221-336-0（平裝）

883.151　　　　　　　　　　　　　98020068

 語言文學類　PG0306

愛之頌

作　　　　者 / 波佩斯古（Elena Liliana Popescu）
中　　　　譯 / 李魁賢
英　　　　譯 / Adrian George Sahlean
發　行　　人 / 宋政坤
執　行　編　輯 / 黃姣潔
圖　文　排　版 / 鄭維心
封　面　設　計 / 陳佩蓉
數　位　轉　譯 / 徐真玉　沈裕閔
圖　書　銷　售 / 林怡君
法　律　顧　問 / 毛國樑　律師
出　版　印　製 / 秀威資訊科技股份有限公司
　　　　　　　台北市內湖區瑞光路583巷25號1樓
　　　　　　　電話：02-2657-9211　傳真：02-2657-9106
　　　　　　　E-mail：service@showwe.com.tw
經　　銷　　商 / 紅螞蟻圖書有限公司
　　　　　　　台北市內湖區舊宗路二段121巷28、32號4樓
　　　　　　　電話：02-2795-3656　傳真：02-2795-4100
　　　　　　　http://www.e-redant.com

2010 年 1 月　BOD 一版
定價：230 元

讀　者　回　函　卡

感謝您購買本書，為提升服務品質，煩請填寫以下問卷，收到您的寶貴意見後，我們會仔細收藏記錄並回贈紀念品，謝謝！

1. 您購買的書名：_____

2. 您從何得知本書的消息？

　□網路書店　□部落格　□資料庫搜尋　□書訊　□電子報　□書店

　□平面媒體　□ 朋友推薦　□網站推薦 □其他_____

3. 您對本書的評價：(請填代號　1.非常滿意 2.滿意 3.尚可 4.再改進)

　封面設計____　版面編排____　內容____　文/譯筆____　價格____

4. 讀完書後您覺得：

　□很有收獲　□有收獲　□收獲不多　□沒收獲

5. 您會推薦本書給朋友嗎？

　□會　□不會，為什麼？_____

6. 其他寶貴的意見：_____

_____

_____

_____

讀者基本資料

姓名：_____　年齡：_____　性別：□女 □男

聯絡電話：_____　E-mail：_____

地址：_____

學歷：□高中(含)以下　　□高中　　□專科學校　　□大學

　　　□研究所(含)以上 □其他_____

職業：□製造業 □金融業 □資訊業 □軍警 □傳播業 □自由業

　　　□服務業 □公務員 □教職　□學生 □其他_____

To：114

台北市內湖區瑞光路 583 巷 25 號 1 樓

秀威資訊科技股份有限公司　　　收

寄件人姓名：

寄件人地址：□□□

(請沿線對摺寄回,謝謝!)

秀威與 BOD

BOD（Books On Demand）是數位出版的大趨勢，秀威資訊率先運用 POD 數位印刷設備來生產書籍，並提供作者全程數位出版服務，致使書籍產銷零庫存，知識傳承不絕版，目前已開闢以下書系：

一、BOD 學術著作—專業論述的閱讀延伸
二、BOD 個人著作—分享生命的心路歷程
三、BOD 旅遊著作—個人深度旅遊文學創作
四、BOD 大陸學者—大陸專業學者學術出版
五、POD 獨家經銷—數位產製的代發行書籍

BOD 秀威網路書店：www.showwe.com.tw
政府出版品網路書店：www.govbooks.com.tw

永不絕版的故事・自己寫・永不休止的音符・自己唱